Hi! My name is Mack.
I'm a Great Pyrenees.
This is Joe.
He's my
human.

MACKS
MOVERS

Joe and I work together.
We own a moving company!

Movers help you
when you're moving
into a new home.

We pack your things,
load them on a truck,
and take them to your
new home for you!

We're very careful with your things.
We make sure nothing gets broken...

RUFF!
LOVERS
...or lost.

MAC
MOVERS

You can trust Joe and me.
We make a good team.

This is the Johnson family.

Today we are helping the Johnsons move.
They are moving from St. Louis
to Kansas City!

It is a big job.
We are going to need help.

This is Joe's brother, Fred.
He will help us today.

There are a lot of things to pack
in the Johnsons' house.

First we pack the kitchen.

I hand the dishes to Joe.
He packs them carefully
in a box.

Next we pack the bedroom.

The Johnsons' cat
has her own special box
for moving!

I carry her carefully
to the truck
so she doesn't get hurt.

Fred needs more packing paper.
I'll bring it!

Whoa!
Look out below!

BANG!

Joe laughs and says
he's glad I'm not hurt.

But now I have to
clean up this mess!

Joe helps me stack the boxes.
He's a great friend.

After all that hard work,
it's time for a lunch break!

Mmm, I love it when Joe packs
chicken sandwiches!

After lunch, we finish
loading the truck.

Soon the whole house is packed!

Joe and Fred
walk through the house
to make sure
nothing was left behind.

I stay to guard the truck.

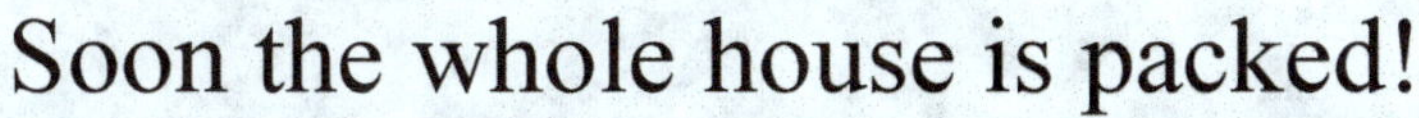

ROFF!

I'm very good at my job.

MACKS
MOVERS
MACKS
MOVERS

The Johnsons' old house
is empty!

Now it's time
to drive the truck
to their new house!

I like to lean my head
out the window
and give directions.

When we arrive, we all work
together to unload the truck.

We take all the boxes and furniture
and put them exactly
where the Johnsons want them.

Soon the truck is empty.

The Johnsons are all moved in!

The Johnsons thank us
for doing a great job.

We wave goodbye.
It's been another
good day at work!

Maybe tomorrow we'll help
your family move!

About the Great Pyrenees

Great Pyrenees are large, calm, independent dogs that were originally bred to guard flocks of sheep in the mountains. Fossilized remains similar to the Great Pyrenees have been found dating back as early as 1000 B.C.! They are big dogs, with the males standing over 28 inches tall and weighing over 100 pounds. They are protective and love to guard their family from intruders.

Meet the Author

Rachel Newhouse is an author and Sunday school teacher from Kansas City, Missouri. She lives with her husband, who is very supportive, and her pit bull, who slept through the creation of this book.

Meet the Illustrator

Patrick Smith has been a doodler from way back and is partially colorblind.

9 781957 432007